W9-BKN-489

This book belongs to

_____

Pollyanna

BY

ELEANOR PORTER

ADAPTED BY MARC D. FALKOFF

❖

■ HARPERFESTIVAL®

A Division of HarperCollins*Publishers*

Pollyanna was first published in 1913.

HarperCollins®, 📖®, and HarperFestival® are registered trademarks
of HarperCollins Publishers Inc.

Pollyanna
Adaptation copyright © 1999 by HarperCollins Publishers Inc.

All rights reserved. No part of this book may be used or reproduced in any manner
whatsoever without written permission except in the case of brief quotations
embodied in critical articles and reviews. Printed in the United States of America.
For information address HarperCollins Children's Books, a division of
HarperCollins Publishers, 10 East 53rd Street, New York, NY 10022.

Library of Congress Cataloging-in-Publication Data
Porter, Eleanor H. (Eleanor Hodgman), 1863–1920.
  Pollyanna / Eleanor Porter ; adapted by Marc D. Falkoff.
    p.   cm.
  Summary: When orphaned eleven-year-old Pollyanna comes to live with austere
and wealthy Aunt Polly, her philosophy of gladness brings happiness to her aunt and
other unhappy members of the community.
  ISBN 0-694-01289-0
  [1. Orphans—Fiction.   2. Aunts—Fiction.   3. Conduct of life—Fiction.]
I. Falkoff, Marc D.   II. Title.   III. Series.
PZ7.P83Po   1999   98-37172
[Fic]—dc21   CIP
                                                                    AC

Typography by Fritz Metsch
1   2   3   4   5   6   7   8   9   10
❖
First Chapter Book Charmers edition, 1999

Visit us on the World Wide Web!
http://www.harperchildrens.com

CONTENTS

❖

Pollyanna

[1]

Pollyanna Arrives

❖

WHEN MISS POLLY received the telegram, she frowned and rang for her maid.

"Nancy," she said, "I want you to prepare the attic room immediately. My niece is arriving today to come live with me. Her father has died, and as I am her only living relation, it is my duty to take her in. She will be arriving on the four o'clock train, and I want you to go meet her there when you've finished."

"Yes, ma'am," said Nancy. "But don't *you* want to—"

Miss Polly cut her off. "No, it is not necessary that I should go myself. Now make haste."

Nancy climbed the stairs to the attic room and looked about with a sigh. Miss Polly was a wealthy woman, and nearly all the rooms in the house were carpeted and hung with fine pictures. But this room held only a bed, two chairs, a washstand, and a small table. And since there were not yet screens for the windows, the room could not be aired out. Nancy neatened up as best she could, then hurried back downstairs.

"Her name is Pollyanna," said Miss Polly, "—a most ridiculous name. My sister named her after our other sister, Anna, and me, though I don't know why. The telegram says she has 'light hair, red-checked dress, and straw hat.' Do you think you can remember that?"

"Yes, ma'am," answered Nancy, who repeated the description over and over to herself on her way to the train station. It was not long before Nancy saw her— the slender little girl in the red-checked dress with two fat braids of hair hanging down her back. Beneath the straw hat an eager, freckled little face turned to the right and to the left, plainly searching the station platform for someone.

"Are you Miss Pollyanna?" Nancy asked the girl. The next moment she found herself half-smothered in a hug.

"Oh, I'm so glad, *glad*, GLAD to see you," cried the eager voice in her ear. "Of course I'm Pollyanna, and I'm so glad you came to meet me! I hoped you would."

"You did?" asked Nancy, wondering how Pollyanna could possibly have known her.

"Oh, yes. And I've been wondering all the way here what you looked like," cried the little girl, dancing on her toes. "And now I know, and I'm glad you look just like you do look."

Nancy was confused, so she just asked the girl if she had a trunk.

"Yes, I have," nodded Pollyanna. "I've got a brand-new one. The Ladies' Aid Society bought it for me, and wasn't it lovely of them?"

They collected her bag and were off at last.

"Oh, isn't this lovely? Is it far? I hope it is. I love to ride," sighed Pollyanna, as the wheels began to turn. "Of course, if it isn't far I won't mind, because I'll be glad to get there all the sooner, you know. What a pretty street! I knew it was going to be pretty. Father told me—"

She stopped with a little choking breath. Nancy saw that Pollyanna's small chin was quivering, and that her eyes were full of tears. But in a moment she hurried on.

"Father told me all about it. And he said I must be glad to come. But it's been pretty hard to do it, because I miss him so. But now I'm sure it'll be easier because I've got you, Aunt Polly. I'm so glad I've got you!"

Nancy's sympathy for the poor little girl suddenly turned into shocked terror.

"Oh, but you've made an awful mistake, dear," she said. "I'm only Nancy. I'm not your Aunt Polly at all!"

"You *aren't*?" cried the surprised little girl. "But who are you?"

"I'm Nancy, your aunt's maid."

Pollyanna relaxed visibly. "Oh, that's all right then." There was a moment's silence, then she went on brightly,

"And do you know? I'm glad, after all, that she didn't come to meet me. Because now I've got her still coming, and I've got you besides."

Soon they arrived at her aunt's house. "Oh, Nancy! It's *beautiful*. I can't *wait* to meet Aunt Polly!"

[2]

The Attic Room

❖

MISS POLLY HARRINGTON did not rise to meet her niece when Nancy and the little girl appeared in the doorway.

"How do you do, Pollyanna? I am your—" But she had no chance to say more. Pollyanna had flown across the room and flung herself into her aunt's lap.

"Oh, Aunt Polly, I don't know how to be glad enough that you let me come to live with you," she cried.

"Yes, yes," said Miss Polly stiffly, trying to unclasp the girl's small, clinging fingers. "Pollyanna, be good enough, please, to stand up straight. I don't know yet what you look like."

Pollyanna drew back at once, laughing. "No, I suppose you don't. But you see I'm not very much to look at, on account of the freckles. Oh, and I ought to explain that Father said—"

"Yes, well, never mind now what your father said,"

interrupted Miss Polly crisply. "You have a trunk, I presume?"

"Oh, yes, Aunt Polly. I haven't got so very much in it—of my own, I mean. But I've got all of Father's books. You see, Father—"

"Pollyanna," interrupted her aunt again sharply, "there is one thing that you might just as well understand right away. And that is, I do not care to have you talking of your father to me."

Pollyanna did not know that her Aunt Polly had never liked her father, because Aunt Polly blamed him for taking her sister away from her.

"Why, Aunt Polly, you mean . . ." She hesitated.

"That is all. We will go upstairs to your room now. Your trunk should already be up there. You may follow me, Pollyanna."

Without speaking, Pollyanna followed her aunt from the room. Her eyes were brimming with tears, but her chin was high.

"After all, I suppose I'm glad she doesn't want me to talk about Father," Pollyanna was thinking. "It'll be easier, maybe, if I *don't* talk about him. Probably that's why she told me not to talk about him."

Pollyanna was on the stairway now. Beneath her feet a marvelous carpet felt soft as moss to her feet. On every side of her were picture frames and lace curtains.

"Oh, Aunt Polly!" cried the little girl. "What a perfectly

lovely house! How awfully glad you must be you're so rich!"

"Certainly not. I hope I'm not too proud to think of myself as rich!"

Miss Polly walked down the hall toward the attic stairway door. She was glad now that she had put the child in the attic room, where this strain of vanity would perhaps be cured.

Eagerly Pollyanna's small feet pattered behind her aunt. Still more eagerly her big blue eyes tried to look in all directions at once. Which beautiful room, full of curtains, rugs, and pictures, was to be hers? Then her aunt opened a door and went up another stairway. Pollyanna followed her to the top.

There was little to be seen here. A bare wall rose on either side, and there were innumerable trunks and boxes stacked up. It was stiflingly hot, too.

Aunt Polly opened a door to a smaller attic room. "Here, Pollyanna, is your room, and there is your trunk. Now, I believe you have everything that you need here. I'll send Nancy up to help you unpack. Supper is at six o'clock," she finished, and left the room.

For a moment after she had gone Pollyanna stood quite still. Then she turned her wide eyes to the bare wall, the bare floor, and the bare windows. She stumbled toward her trunk and fell on her knees, covering her face with her hands.

Nancy found her like that a few minutes later. "There, there, you poor lamb," she crooned. "I was afraid I'd find you like this."

"I'm all right, Nancy. I was just missing Father terribly," sobbed the little girl.

"Come, let's open this trunk and take out your dresses."

Tearfully, Pollyanna opened the trunk. "There aren't very many there," she said.

"Then they're all the sooner unpacked," declared Nancy.

Pollyanna gave a sudden smile. "That's so! I can be glad of that, can't I!"

Nancy stared. "Why, of course, I guess."

So they began to unpack and settle into the room. "I'm sure it's going to be a very nice room. Don't you think so?" Pollyanna asked after a while.

There was no answer. Nancy was very busy, apparently, with her head in the trunk.

"I can be glad there isn't any mirror here, too, because where there isn't any mirror I can't see my freckles."

Still Nancy said nothing. At one of the windows, a few minutes later, Pollyanna gave a cry and clapped her hands joyously.

"Oh, Nancy, I hadn't seen this before," she breathed. "Look, over there. Those trees and the houses and that lovely church spire, and the river shining just like silver.

Why, Nancy, nobody needs pictures with *that* to look at. Oh, I'm so glad now Aunt Polly let me have this room!"

Luckily for Nancy, who was about to tell Pollyanna just what she thought of Aunt Polly giving her niece this room, at just that moment Miss Polly's bell rang, and she ran downstairs without having to say a word.

Left alone, Pollyanna went back to her "picture," as she now thought of her view from the window. After a time, though, she could no longer stand the stifling heat. She went to open the window, and the next moment she was leaning far out, drinking in the fresh, sweet air.

Then she ran to the other window. That, too, soon flew open. A big fly swept past her nose and buzzed noisily about the room. Then another came, and another. But Pollyanna paid no heed. She had made a wonderful discovery: a huge tree flung great branches at this window.

The next moment she had climbed to the window ledge. From there it was easy to step to the nearest tree branch. Then, like a monkey, she swung herself from limb to limb until she reached the lowest branch and dropped to the ground, landing on all fours in the soft grass.

Fifteen minutes later the great clock in the hallway of Miss Polly's house struck six. At precisely the last stroke Nancy sounded the bell for supper.

One, two, three minutes passed. Miss Polly frowned. Then she swept into the dining room.

"Nancy," she said, "my niece is late. I told her what time supper was, and now she will have to suffer the consequences. She may as well begin at once to learn to be punctual. When she comes down, she may have bread and milk in the kitchen."

"Yes, ma'am," Nancy said.

Right after supper Nancy crept up to the attic room.

"Bread and milk, indeed!" she was muttering as she softly pushed open the door. But the next moment she gave a frightened cry. "Pollyanna! Where are you?" She looked in the closet, under the bed, and even in the trunk, but Pollyanna was nowhere at all.

3

The Glad Game

❖

"MISS POLLYANNA, WHAT a scare you gave me!" cried Nancy when Pollyanna came in a few minutes later by the kitchen door. Luckily, Nancy hadn't yet told Miss Polly that her niece was missing.

"Oh, I'm so sorry, Nancy. I was out in the garden exploring."

"But I didn't even know you left," said Nancy. "Nobody saw you go. I guess you flew right up through the roof!"

Pollyanna skipped gleefully. "I did, almost. Only I flew *down* instead of up. I came down the tree."

"Hunh! I wonder what Miss Polly'd say to *that!*" thought Nancy to herself.

Pollyanna was looking about the kitchen. "You must be hungry," said Nancy. "I'm afraid you'll have to have bread and milk in the kitchen with me. Your aunt didn't like it that you didn't come down to supper, you know."

"But I couldn't. I was outside."

"Yes. But she didn't know that," said Nancy. "I'm sorry about the bread and milk, dear."

"Oh, I'm not. I'm glad."

"Glad? Why?"

"Why, I like bread and milk, and I'd like to eat with you. I don't see any trouble about being glad about that."

"You don't seem to have any trouble being glad about anything," said Nancy.

Pollyanna laughed softly. "Well, that's the game, you know."

"The game?"

"Yes. The Glad Game."

"Whatever in the world are you talking about?"

"Why, it's a game. Father taught it to me, and it's lovely. We've played it always, ever since I was a little girl. We began it when we got some crutches in a care package."

"*Crutches?*"

"Yes. You see, I'd wanted a doll. But when the package came, the lady wrote that they didn't have any dolls, but they did have these little crutches. So she sent them along in case I needed them sometime. And that's when we began it."

"Well, I can't see any game about that," declared Nancy.

"Oh, yes. The game is to find something about everything to be glad about, no matter what it is," replied Pollyanna. "And we began right then, on the crutches."

"Well, goodness me! I can't see anything to be glad about getting a pair of crutches when you wanted a doll!"

Pollyanna clapped her hands. "Oh, there is! But I couldn't see it either, Nancy, at first. Father had to tell it to me."

"Well, then, suppose you tell *me*."

"Goosey! Why, just be glad because *you don't need them!*" cried out Pollyanna. "You see, it's easy when you know how!"

"Well, I'll be!" said Nancy.

"We've played it ever since," continued Pollyanna. "And the harder it is, the more fun. Only sometimes it's almost too hard, like when your father goes to heaven."

"Well, I don't know that *I* could play that game," thought Nancy, shaking her head slowly.

Pollyanna ate her bread and milk with good appetite. Then she went into the sitting room, where her aunt was reading. Miss Polly looked up coldly.

"I'm very sorry, Pollyanna, to have been obliged so soon to send you into the kitchen to eat bread and milk."

"But I was real glad you did it, Aunt Polly. I like

bread and milk, and Nancy, too. You mustn't feel bad about that one bit." Then Pollyanna came straight to her aunt's side and gave her a big hug. "I've had such a beautiful time, so far. I know I'm going to just *love* living with you. Good night, Aunt Polly." She left the room and went upstairs.

"What a most extraordinary child!" said Miss Polly. She didn't know if she should laugh or cry.

4

Aunt Polly's Duty

❖

IT WAS NEARLY seven o'clock when Pollyanna awoke the next morning.

The little room was cooler now, and the air blew in fresh and sweet. Outside, the birds were twittering, and Pollyanna flew to the window to talk to them. She saw then that down in the garden her aunt was already out among the rose bushes.

Down the attic stairs sped Pollyanna, leaving both doors wide open. Through the hall, down the next flight, then bang through the front door and around to the garden she ran.

Aunt Polly was leaning over a rose bush when Pollyanna flung herself upon her.

"Oh, Aunt Polly, I'm so glad this morning just to be alive!"

"Pollyanna!" said her aunt sternly. "Is this the usual way you say good morning?"

The little girl dropped to her toes and danced lightly up and down.

"No, only when I love folks so much that I just can't help it! I saw you from my window, Aunt Polly, and you looked so good I just had to come down and hug you!"

Miss Polly attempted to frown, but not with her usual success. "Pollyanna, it's breakfast time," she finally said.

Breakfast, for the first five minutes, was a silent meal. Then Miss Polly, watching the flight of two flies darting here and there over the table, said sternly, "Nancy, where did those flies come from?"

"I don't know, ma'am."

"I reckon maybe they're my flies, Aunt Polly," observed Pollyanna cheerfully. "There were lots of them this morning having a beautiful time upstairs."

"Yours!" gasped Miss Polly. "What do you mean? Where did they come from?"

"Why, from outdoors, of course, through the windows. I saw some of them come in."

"You saw them? You mean you raised those windows without any screens?"

"Yes. There weren't any screens there, Aunt Polly."

"Pollyanna, I have ordered screens for those windows. I knew, of course, that it was my duty to do that. But it seems to me that you have quite forgotten *your* duty."

16

"My duty?" Pollyanna's eyes were wide with wonder.

"Certainly. I know it is warm, but I consider it your duty to keep your windows closed till those screens come. Flies, Pollyanna, are not only unclean and annoying, but very dangerous to health. After breakfast, I will give you a little pamphlet on this matter to read."

"To read? Oh, *thank you*, Aunt Polly. I love to read!"

Miss Polly drew in her breath, and Pollyanna, seeing her stern face, said, "Of course I'm sorry about the duty I forgot, Aunt Polly," she said. "I'll close the windows after breakfast."

Her aunt made no reply. When the meal was over, she went to the bookcase, took out a small booklet, and came to her niece's side.

"This is the article I spoke of, Pollyanna. I desire you to go to your room at once and read it. I will be up in half an hour to look over your things."

Pollyanna, her eyes on the illustration of a fly's head, cried joyously, "Oh, thank you, Aunt Polly!" The next moment she skipped merrily from the room, banging the door behind her.

Half an hour later, when Miss Polly climbed the stairs and entered Pollyanna's room, she was greeted with a burst of enthusiasm.

"Oh, Aunt Polly, I never saw anything so perfectly lovely and interesting in my life! I'm so glad you gave me that book to read. Why, I didn't suppose flies could carry such a lot of things on their feet, and—"

"That will do," said Aunt Polly. "Pollyanna, you may bring out your clothes now, and I will look them over and decide what is fit for you to keep."

Pollyanna laid down the pamphlet and turned toward the closet.

When Aunt Polly was through inspecting the clothes, she said, "In the fall you will enter school here. Meanwhile, I suppose I ought to hear you read aloud half an hour each day."

"I love to read. But if you don't want to hear me, I'd be glad just to read to myself."

"I don't doubt it," responded Miss Polly. "Have you studied music?"

"I can play the piano a little. But I'd just as soon let that go as not, Aunt Polly."

"Very likely," observed Aunt Polly. "Nevertheless, I think it is my duty to see that you are properly instructed in at least the basics of music. You do not know how to cook, I presume."

Pollyanna laughed. "Some of the Ladies' Aiders tried to teach me, but we only got to chocolate fudge and fig cake!"

"Chocolate fudge and fig cake, indeed!" said Miss Polly. "This is to be your schedule. At nine o'clock every morning you will read aloud one half-hour to me. You will use the time before that to put this room in order. Wednesday and Saturday mornings you will spend with Nancy in the kitchen, learning to cook. Other mornings you will sew with me. That will leave the afternoons for your music."

Pollyanna cried out in dismay, "Oh, but Aunt Polly, you haven't left any time at all to *live*."

"To live, child! What do you mean? As if you weren't living all the time!"

"Oh, of course I'd be *breathing* all the time I was doing those things, Aunt Polly, but I wouldn't be living. I mean *living*—doing the things you want to do, like playing outdoors, reading, climbing hills, and finding out all about the houses and the people and everything everywhere. That's what I call living, Aunt Polly."

"You *are* the most extraordinary child! You will be allowed a proper amount of playtime, of course. But if I am willing to do my duty by educating you, you ought not to be ungrateful."

Pollyanna looked shocked. "Oh, Aunt Polly, as if I ever could be ungrateful to *you*! Why, I *love* you!"

Miss Polly blushed, but said sternly, "Very well. Then see that you don't act ungratefully."

She had gone halfway down the stairs when a small, unsteady voice called after her, "Please, Aunt Polly, you didn't tell me which of my things you wanted to give away."

"Not one of your dresses is fit for my niece to wear. I would not be doing my duty by you if I let you go out in any one of them. We'll drive into town this afternoon and get you new ones."

Pollyanna sighed now. She believed she was going to hate that word *duty*.

"Aunt Polly, please," she called. "Isn't there any way you can be *glad* about all that—that *duty* business?"

"What?" Miss Polly looked up in surprise. "Don't be impertinent, Pollyanna!"

5

Pollyanna's Punishment

❖

THAT AFTERNOON MISS Polly and her niece drove to town. They spent a long time shopping, and when it was over Pollyanna was exhausted.

At half past eight Pollyanna went up to bed. But the screens had not yet come, and the little room was like an oven. Pollyanna looked at the two closed windows, but she did not raise them.

Just how long she lay in sleepless misery, tossing from side to side in the hot little cot, she did not know. But it seemed to her that it must have been hours before she finally slipped out of bed, felt her way across the room, and opened her door.

Out in the main attic all was velvet blackness. Pollyanna pattered straight across the attic to the window. She had hoped that this window might have a screen, but it did not. Outside, however, there was a wide world of moonlit beauty.

As she peered out, she saw that only a little way below the window was the wide, flat roof of Aunt Polly's room. If only she were out there in the moonlight and cool, fresh air!

Suddenly Pollyanna remembered that she had seen in the attic a row of long white bags that Nancy said held the winter clothing. Pollyanna felt her way to these bags, selected a nice fat soft one for a bed, and a thinner one for a pillow. Then she pattered to the moonlit window again, raised the sash, stuffed the bags through to the roof below, and let herself down after it, closing the window carefully behind her.

How deliciously cool it was outside! Pollyanna danced up and down with delight, drawing in long, full breaths of the refreshing air. And the roof was so broad and flat that she had no fear of falling off. Finally she curled herself up on the makeshift mattress, arranged the bag for a pillow, and settled herself to sleep.

"I'm so glad now that the screens didn't come," she murmured, blinking up at the stars. "Else I couldn't have done this!"

But downstairs in her own room Miss Polly was pale and frightened. "Nancy," she called. "Come quickly! Somebody is on the roof. He may be a robber! Hurry, hurry!"

Soon Pollyanna was abruptly awakened by a lantern flash. She opened her eyes to find Aunt Polly and Nancy peering out the attic window at her.

"*Pollyanna!* What on earth are you doing up here?" cried Aunt Polly.

Pollyanna blinked sleepy eyes and sat up. "Aunt Polly! Nancy! Don't look so scared. It's only that I was so hot in my room. But I shut the window, Aunt Polly, so the flies couldn't get in."

"Pollyanna, hand those things to me at once and come in here. Of all the extraordinary children!" she said.

To Pollyanna the air inside was all the more stifling after that cool breath of the outside. But she did not complain.

At the top of the stairs Miss Polly said, "For the rest of the night, Pollyanna, you are to sleep in my bed with me. The screens will be here tomorrow, but until then I consider it my duty to keep you where I can see you."

Pollyanna drew in her breath. "With you? In your bed?" she cried. "Oh, Aunt Polly, how perfectly lovely of you!"

There was no reply. Miss Polly, to tell the truth, was feeling curiously helpless. For the third time since Pollyanna's arrival, she was punishing Pollyanna, and for the third time her punishment was being taken as a special reward!

6

Pollyanna Pays a Visit

❖

IT WAS NOT long before life at Miss Polly's house settled into something like order. Pollyanna sewed, practiced, read aloud, and studied cooking in the kitchen. Nonetheless, she had plenty of time to "just live."

Almost every pleasant afternoon found Pollyanna begging for an errand to run, so that she might be off for a walk in one direction or another.

One particular day Pollyanna was carrying calf's-foot jelly to Mrs. Snow, who was an invalid. Miss Polly always sent Nancy once a week to take something to Mrs. Snow, but today Pollyanna had begged her aunt to let her go. Miss Polly said she could.

"I'm glad that *I* don't have to go," Nancy told Pollyanna, "but it's a shame *you* have to!"

"But I'd love to do it, Nancy. I just love people!"

"Well, you won't after you've done it once," predicted Nancy.

"Why not?"

"Because she's *cantankerous*."

"But why, Nancy?"

Nancy shrugged her shoulders. "Well, in plain words, it's just that nothing is ever right to her. If you take her jelly, you're sure to hear she wants chicken, but if you *do* bring her chicken, she'll just hanker for lamb broth!"

"Why, what a funny woman!" laughed Pollyanna.

She walked to the gate of Mrs. Snow's little cottage, and at her knock Mrs. Snow's daughter came to the door, and then brought Pollyanna into the sickroom.

The girl closed the door, leaving Pollyanna to blink a little before she could see in the gloom. Then she saw a woman half-sitting up in the bed across the room.

"How do you do, Mrs. Snow? Aunt Polly says she hopes you are comfortable today, and she's sent you some calf's-foot jelly."

"Dear me! Jelly?" murmured the woman. "Of course I'm very much obliged, but I was hoping it would be lamb broth today."

Pollyanna frowned. "I thought it was *chicken* you wanted when folks brought you jelly."

"What?" The sick woman turned sharply.

"Why, nothing," said Pollyanna. "And of course it

doesn't really make any difference. It's only that Nancy said it was chicken you wanted when we brought jelly, and lamb broth when we brought chicken."

The sick woman pulled herself up in the bed. "Well, Miss Impertinence, who are you?"

"Oh, *that* isn't my name, Mrs. Snow, and I'm so glad it isn't, too! I'm Pollyanna Whittier, Miss Polly Harrington's niece, and I've come to live with her. That's why I'm here with the jelly this morning."

At the reference to the jelly Mrs. Snow fell back on her pillow.

"Very well. Thank you. Your aunt is very kind, of course, but my appetite isn't very good this morning, and I was wanting lamb—" She stopped suddenly. "Here, go to that window and pull up the curtain. I'd like to know what you look like!"

"Oh, dear, then you'll see my freckles, won't you?" Pollyanna sighed, as she went to the window. "And just when I was so glad it was dark and you couldn't see them. There! Now you can—Oh!" she broke off excitedly, as she turned back to the bed, "I'm so glad you wanted to see me, because now I can see you. They didn't tell me you were so pretty!"

"Me, pretty?" cried the woman. "Nonsense."

"Oh, but your eyes are so big and dark, and your hair's wonderfully curly," cooed Pollyanna. "I love curls. Why, Mrs. Snow, you are *so* pretty! I should think you'd know it when you looked at yourself in the mirror. Just let me show you." And she skipped over to the bureau and picked up a small hand mirror.

On the way back to the bed she stopped, looking carefully at the sick woman.

"I reckon maybe, if you don't mind, I'd like to fix your hair just a little before I let you see it," she said. "May I fix your hair, please?"

"Why, I suppose so, if you want to," answered Mrs. Snow.

"Oh, thank you. I love to fix people's hair," said Pollyanna, reaching for a comb. "I won't do much today, I'm in such a hurry for you to see how nice you look."

Pollyanna worked swiftly, combing curls into fluffiness, and teasing and brushing Mrs. Snow's hair. Meanwhile, the sick woman couldn't help tingling with excitement.

"There!" cried Pollyanna. "Now we're ready to be looked at!" And she held out the mirror.

"Humph!" said the sick woman, looking at her reflection. "It *is* nice. But it won't last."

"Of course not, and I'm glad, too," laughed Pollyanna cheerfully. "Because then I can fix it all over again. Oh, I'd *love* curly hair like yours!"

"Well, you wouldn't! Not if you were me. You wouldn't be glad for curly hair, or anything else, if you had to lie here all day as I do!"

"Why, it would be kind of hard to do, wouldn't it?" said Pollyanna thoughtfully.

"Do what?"

"Be glad about things."

"Be glad about things, when you're sick in bed all your days? Well, I should say it would," said Mrs. Snow. "Just try to tell me something to be glad about!"

To Mrs. Snow's amazement, Pollyanna sprang to her feet and clapped her hands.

"Oh, goody! That'll be a hard one, won't it? I've got to go now, but I'll think and think all the way home, and maybe the next time I come I can tell it to you. Good-bye. I've had a lovely time. Good-bye," she called again, as she tripped through the doorway.

"Well! What an unusual girl!" muttered Mrs. Snow, staring after her visitor. "But she *has* got a knack with hair, that's for sure. I didn't know I could look so pretty. Humph!"

7

The Man

❖

DURING POLLYANNA'S MANY walks she often passed a stranger whom she soon thought of as "the Man." The Man wore a long black coat and a high silk hat. He was rather pale, and his hair was somewhat gray. He was always alone, which made Pollyanna feel a little sorry for him. So one day she decided to speak to him.

"How do you do, sir? Isn't this a nice day?" she called cheerily as she approached him.

The Man threw a hurried glance about him, then stopped uncertainly.

"Did you speak to me?" he asked in a sharp voice.

"Yes, sir," beamed Pollyanna. "I say, it's a nice day, isn't it?"

"Eh? Oh! Humph!" he grunted, and strode on again.

Pollyanna laughed. He was such a funny man, she thought.

The next day she saw him again. "It isn't quite so nice as yesterday, but it's pretty nice," she called out cheerfully.

"Eh? Oh! Humph!" grunted the Man as before.

When for the third time Pollyanna called to him in much the same manner, the Man stopped abruptly.

"See here, child, who are you, and why are you speaking to me every day?"

"I'm Pollyanna Whittier, and I thought you looked lonesome. I'm so glad you stopped. Now we're introduced, only I don't know your name yet."

"Well, of all the—" The Man did not finish his sentence, but strode on faster than ever.

"Maybe he didn't understand," Pollyanna thought. "That was only half an introduction. I don't know *his* name yet."

It was raining the next time Pollyanna saw the Man.

"It isn't so nice today, is it?" she called out gaily. "I'm glad it doesn't rain always, anyhow!"

The Man stopped abruptly. There was an angry scowl on his face.

"See here, little girl, we might just as well settle this thing right now," he began. "I've got something besides the weather to think of. I don't know whether the sun shines or not."

Pollyanna beamed joyously. "No, sir. I thought you didn't. That's why I told you."

"Yes. Well, eh? What?" he broke off sharply.

"That's why I told you, so you would notice it, you know, that the sun shines, and all that. I knew you'd be glad it did if you only stopped to think of it, and you didn't look a bit as if you *were* thinking of it!"

"Well, of all the——" started the Man. "See here, why don't you find someone your own age to talk to?"

"I'd like to, sir, but there aren't any around here. Still, I don't mind so very much. I like old folks just as well, maybe better, sometimes."

"Well, of all the——" he said again, and he turned and walked on as before.

The next time Pollyanna met the Man, his eyes were gazing straight into hers, with a directness that made his face look really pleasant, Pollyanna thought.

"Good afternoon," he greeted her a little stiffly. "Perhaps I'd better say right away that I *know* the sun is shining today."

"But you don't have to tell me," nodded Pollyanna brightly. "I *knew* you knew it just as soon as I saw you."

"Oh, you did, did you?"

"Yes, sir. I saw it in your eyes, you know, and in your smile."

"Humph!" grunted the Man as he passed on.

The Man always spoke to Pollyanna after this, and often he spoke first, though usually he said little but "Good afternoon." Even that, however, was a great surprise to Nancy, who happened to be with Pollyanna one day when the greeting was given.

"Miss Pollyanna," she gasped, "did that man *speak* to you?"

"Why, yes, he always does now," smiled Pollyanna.

"He always does! Goodness! Do you know who he is?" asked Nancy.

Pollyanna frowned and shook her head. "I reckon he forgot to tell me one day. You see, I did my part of the introducing, but he didn't."

"But he never speaks to *anybody*. He hasn't for years, I guess, except when he has to, for business, and all that. He's John Pendleton. He lives all by himself in the big house on Pendleton Hill."

"But why doesn't he talk with anybody?" Pollyanna asked.

"He's just not a friendly man," said Nancy.

"Well, I'm glad he speaks to me."

8

A Surprise for Mrs. Snow

❋

THE NEXT WEEK Pollyanna went to see Mrs. Snow again.

Pollyanna came cheerily into the room, setting her basket carefully down on a chair. "My! But isn't it dark in here? I can't see you a bit." So she crossed over to the window and pulled up the shade. "I want to see if you've fixed your hair like I did. Oh, you haven't! But never mind, we'll get to it later. But now I want you to see what I've brought you."

The woman stirred restlessly. "Well, what is it?"

"Guess! What do you want?" Pollyanna had skipped back to the basket.

The sick woman hesitated. She did not realize it herself, but she was so used to wanting what she did not have, that to say what she *did* want seemed impossible.

"Well, of course, there's lamb broth—"

"I've got it!" crowed Pollyanna.

"But that's what I *didn't* want," sighed the sick woman, sure now of what her stomach craved. "It was chicken I wanted."

"Oh, I've got that, too!" chuckled Pollyanna.

The woman turned in amazement. "*Both* of them?"

"Yes, and calf's-foot jelly, too!" shouted Pollyanna. "I was just bound you should have what you wanted for once, so Nancy and I fixed it. I'm so glad you did want chicken."

There was no reply.

"There! I'm to leave them all," announced Pollyanna as she arranged the three bowls in a row on the table. "Like enough it'll be lamb broth you want tomorrow. How do you do today?"

"Very poorly, thank you," murmured Mrs. Snow. "I couldn't sleep at all this morning. Nellie Higgins next door has begun music lessons, and her practicing drives me crazy."

Polly nodded sympathetically. "I know. It must be awful!" But suddenly Pollyanna clapped her hands. "Oh! I almost forgot. I've thought it up, Mrs. Snow—what you can be glad about."

"Oh!" scoffed the woman. "Yes, I remember that. But I didn't suppose you would."

"Oh, yes," nodded Pollyanna. "And I found it, too.

But it was hard. It's all the more fun, though, when it is hard."

"Well, what is it?"

Pollyanna drew a long breath. "I thought how glad you could be that other folks weren't like you, all sick in bed like this, you know," she announced.

Mrs. Snow stared. Her eyes were angry. "Well, really!" she said.

"And now I'll tell you the game," proposed Pollyanna. "It'll be just lovely for you to play. You see, it's like this." And she began to tell of the care package, and the crutches, and the game she and her father used to play.

The story was just finished when Mrs. Snow's daughter appeared at the door.

"Your aunt wants you, Miss Pollyanna," she said. "She telephoned and says you're to hurry, that you've got some practicing to make up before dark."

Pollyanna rose reluctantly. "All right," she sighed. "I'll hurry." Then she said, "I suppose I ought to be glad I've got legs to hurry with, hadn't I, Mrs. Snow?"

There was no answer. Mrs. Snow's eyes were closed. But there were tears on her cheeks.

"Good-bye," said Pollyanna over her shoulder, as she reached the door. "I'm awfully sorry about the hair, I wanted to do it. But maybe I can next time!"

[9]

Pollyanna's New Room

❖

LATER THAT AFTERNOON, Pollyanna was coming down from her attic room when she met her aunt on the stairs.

"Why, Aunt Polly, how perfectly lovely!" she cried. "You were coming up to see me! Come right in. I love company."

Now Miss Polly had not been intending to call on her niece. She had been looking for a wool shawl in the cedar chest. But to her surprise, she now found herself in Pollyanna's little room, sitting in one of the straight-backed chairs.

"I love company," said Pollyanna. "And of course now I just love this room, even if it hasn't got the carpets and curtains and pictures that I'd—" With a blush Pollyanna stopped short.

"What's that, Pollyanna?"

"N-nothing, Aunt Polly, truly. I didn't mean to say it."

"Perhaps not," said Miss Polly coldly. "But you did say it, so suppose you finish."

"But it was only that I'd been kind of planning on pretty carpets and lace curtains and things, you know. But, of course—"

"*Planning* on them!" cried Miss Polly sharply.

Pollyanna blushed again. "I shouldn't have, of course, Aunt Polly," she apologized. "It was only because I'd always wanted them and hadn't had them, I suppose. But truly, Aunt Polly, it wasn't at all long before I was glad that the bureau *didn't* have a looking glass, because it didn't show my freckles, and there couldn't be a nicer picture than the one out my window there. And you've been so good to me that—"

Miss Polly rose suddenly to her feet. Her face was very red. "That will do, Pollyanna," she said. "You have said quite enough, I'm sure." The next minute she had swept down the stairs.

That evening Miss Polly said to Nancy, "You may move Pollyanna's things downstairs tomorrow morning. I've decided to have my niece sleep in the room next to mine for now."

"Yes, ma'am," said Nancy, in disbelief. What in the world had come over Miss Polly?

A minute later Nancy told Pollyanna the news, and the girl actually grew white. "Really, Nancy? Really and truly?"

But instead of waiting for an answer, Pollyanna flew to her aunt's room. *Bang* went two doors and a chair before Pollyanna at last reached her goal.

"Oh, Aunt Polly. Did you mean it, really? Why, that room's got *everything,* the carpet and curtains and three pictures, besides the one outdoors, too, because the windows look the same way. Oh, Aunt Polly!"

"Very well, Pollyanna. I am happy that you like the change. But you must take proper care of the room." Miss Polly spoke sternly, though for some reason she felt inclined to cry.

10

An Adventure in Pendleton Woods

❖

ONE WARM DAY in early June, Pollyanna was taking a walk through the green quiet of Pendleton Woods. Suddenly she lifted her head and listened. A dog had barked some distance ahead. A moment later he came dashing toward her, still barking.

"Hello, doggie, hello!" Pollyanna snapped her fingers at the dog and looked expectantly down the path. She had seen the dog once before, she was sure. He had been with the Man, Mr. John Pendleton. For some minutes she waited, but the Man did not appear. Then she turned back to the dog.

The dog was acting strangely. He was still barking, and he was running back and forth, back and forth, in the path ahead.

All at once Pollyanna realized that something was wrong, and she followed the dog when he dashed madly ahead. It was not long before Pollyanna came upon the reason for it all: the Man, lying at the foot of a steep rock a few yards from the path!

With a cry, Pollyanna ran to his side. "Mr. Pendleton! Oh, are you hurt?"

"Hurt? Oh, no! I'm just taking a nap in the sunshine," he snapped. "Yes, of course I'm hurt. See here, have you got any sense?"

Pollyanna caught her breath. "Why, Mr. Pendleton, most of the Ladies' Aiders thought I had real good sense. I heard them say so one day when—"

The Man smiled and stopped her. "There, there, child, I beg your pardon. It's only that my leg is terribly hurt. Now listen." He paused, and with some difficulty reached his hand into his trousers pocket and brought out a key. "Straight through the path there, about five minutes' walk, is my house. This key will let you in. When you get into the house, go straight through the hall to the telephone. Do you know how to use a telephone?"

"Oh, yes, sir! Why, once when Aunt Polly—"

"Never mind Aunt Polly now," cut in Mr. Pendleton. "Hunt up Dr. Thomas Chilton's number on the card you'll find somewhere around there. Tell him that John Pendleton is at the foot of Little Eagle Ledge with a broken leg, and to come at once with a stretcher and two men."

"A broken leg? Oh, Mr. Pendleton, how perfectly

awful!" shuddered Pollyanna. "But I'm so glad I came. Can I do anything to—"

"Yes, you can, but not if you stay *here*."

With a little sob, Pollyanna started for the house, keeping her eyes on the ground to make sure that no twig or stone tripped her hurrying feet.

It was not long before she came in sight of the house. She sped across the big lawn, fit the key into the lock, and swung the door open.

She ran to the telephone, found Dr. Chilton's number, and in due time she had Dr. Chilton himself on the line. She delivered her message, then hung up the receiver and ran out of the house. In what seemed an incredibly short time, Pollyanna was back by the Man's side.

"Well, what's the trouble? Couldn't you get in?" he demanded.

Pollyanna opened wide her eyes. "Why, of course I could! I'm *here*, aren't I? As if I'd be here if I hadn't got in! And the doctor will be right up just as soon as possible with the men and things. He said he knew just where you were, so I rushed back to be with you."

"Did you?" smiled the Man. "Well, I should think you might find pleasanter companions."

"Do you mean because you're so cross?"

"Thanks for your frankness. Yes."

Pollyanna laughed. "But you're only cross *outside,* you aren't cross inside a bit!"

"Indeed! How do you know that?"

"Oh, lots of ways. There, like that, the way you act with the dog," she added, pointing to his hand resting on the dog's head near him. "It's funny how dogs and cats know the insides of folks better than other folks do, isn't it?"

In a short time the dog pricked up his ears and whined softly. The next moment Pollyanna heard voices, and very soon three men appeared, carrying a stretcher.

The tallest of them, a kind-eyed man whom Pollyanna knew by sight as Dr. Chilton, walked up cheerily. "Well, my little lady, are you playing nurse?"

"Oh, no, sir," smiled Pollyanna. "I haven't given him a bit of medicine. But I'm glad I was here."

"So am I," nodded the doctor as he turned his attention to the injured man.

"So am I," said Mr. Pendleton.

11

Dr. Chilton

✤

IT WAS ABOUT a week after the accident in the woods
that Pollyanna made her second visit to the house of Mr.
Pendleton.

This time Pollyanna rang the bell. Before long a maid
opened the door.

"If you please, I've brought some calf's-foot jelly for
Mr. Pendleton," smiled Pollyanna.

"Thank you," said the maid, reaching for the bowl.
"Who shall I say sent it? And it's calf's-foot jelly, you
say?"

Dr. Chilton, coming into the hall at that moment,
saw the disappointed look on Pollyanna's face. He
stepped quickly forward. "Ah! Some calf's-foot jelly," he
said. "That will be fine! Maybe you'd like to see our
patient, eh?"

"Oh, yes, sir," beamed Pollyanna.

"But Doctor, didn't Mr. Pendleton give orders not to admit anyone?" the maid asked.

"Oh, yes," nodded the doctor. "But this little girl is better than a bottle of medicine for him any day. If anybody can take the grouch out of Mr. Pendleton this afternoon, she can."

The maid directed Pollyanna to Mr. Pendleton's room, and then announced the girl's presence. "Sir, here's a little girl with some jelly. The doctor said I was to bring her in."

The next moment Pollyanna found herself alone with a very cross-looking man lying flat on his back in bed.

"See here, didn't I say—" began an angry voice. "Oh, it's you!"

"Yes, sir," smiled Pollyanna. "I'm so glad they let me in! You see, at first the lady almost took my jelly, and I was so afraid I wasn't going to see you at all. Then the doctor came, and he said I might. Wasn't he lovely to let me see you?"

In spite of himself, the Man smiled.

"And I've brought you some jelly," resumed Pollyanna. "Calf's-foot. Do you like it?"

"Never ate it." The smile had gone, and the scowl had come back to the Man's face.

"Didn't you? Well, if you didn't, then you can't know you *don't* like it, anyhow, can you? So I reckon I'm glad you haven't, after all. Now, if you knew—"

"Yes, yes. Well, there's one thing I know all right, and that is that I'm flat on my back right here this minute, and that I'm liable to stay here forever."

Pollyanna looked shocked. "Oh, no! It couldn't be forever. Broken legs don't last. It's not like being a lifelong invalid, you know. I should think you could be glad of that. And you only broke one. You can be glad it wasn't two," added Pollyanna.

"Of course! I'm so fortunate," sniffed the Man. "Looking at it from that standpoint, I suppose I should be glad I wasn't a centipede and didn't break fifty!"

Pollyanna chuckled. "Oh, that's the best yet!"

In spite of himself, Mr. Pendleton couldn't help laughing. "What an extraordinary girl you are!" he said. "And now I need some rest, little one."

As Pollyanna left the house, Dr. Chilton walked up to her. "Well, Miss Pollyanna, may I have the pleasure of seeing you home?" he asked smilingly.

"Thank you, sir. I just love to ride," beamed Pollyanna.

"Do you?" smiled the doctor. "Well, as near as I can judge, there are a good many things you 'love' to do, eh?" he added as they drove briskly away.

"Why, I don't know. I reckon perhaps there are. I like to do most everything that's *living*. Of course, I don't like the other things very well, sewing and reading out loud, and all that. But *they* aren't *living*."

"No? What are they, then?"

"Aunt Polly says they're 'learning to live,'" sighed Pollyanna.

The doctor smiled a little oddly. "Does she? Well, I should think she might say just that."

"Yes," said Pollyanna. "But I don't see it that way at all. I don't think you have to *learn* how to live."

The doctor drew a long sigh. "I'm afraid some of us do have to, little girl," he said. Then for a time he was silent. Pollyanna felt sorry for him. He looked so sad.

"Dr. Chilton, I should think being a doctor would be the very gladdest kind of business there was."

The doctor turned in surprise. "Gladdest! When I see so much suffering always, everywhere I go?" he cried.

She nodded. "I know. But you're *helping* it, don't you see? And of course you're glad to help it! And so that makes you the gladdest of any of us, all the time."

The doctor's eyes suddenly filled with tears. He had no wife and no children, so his profession was very dear to him. "Thank you, Pollyanna," he said, with the bright smile his patients knew and loved so well.

When they arrived at Miss Polly's, the doctor left Pollyanna at her own door and drove rapidly away.

Pollyanna found her aunt in the sitting room.

"Who was that man, the one who drove into the yard, Pollyanna?" asked Aunt Polly.

"Why, Aunt Polly, that was Dr. Chilton! Don't you know him?"

"Dr. Chilton! What was he doing here?"

"He drove me home. Oh, and I gave the jelly to Mr. Pendleton, and—"

"But Dr. Chilton! I mean, why did he. . . . Why was. . . . Was he. . . . I must go rest," she said at last.

Pollyanna watched in bewilderment as her tongue-tied aunt stumbled up the stairs.

12

Dressing Up Aunt Polly

❖

IT WAS ON a rainy day about a week later that Miss Polly went out for a walk. When she returned, her cheeks were a bright, pretty pink, and her hair, blown by the damp wind, had fluffed into kinks and curls.

Pollyanna had never before seen her aunt look like this. "Why, she's really quite young!" she thought.

What she said, though, was, "Oh! Why, Aunt Polly, you've got *curls*! Oh, Aunt Polly, they're so pretty!"

"Nonsense!"

"But it isn't nonsense," said Pollyanna. "You don't know how pretty you look with your hair like that!"

"Pollyanna!" Miss Polly spoke sharply, but Pollyanna's words had given her an odd throb of joy. When was the last time anybody cared how she looked?

"Oh, Aunt Polly, will you let me do your hair?"

Aunt Polly put her hand to her throat, but she didn't say anything.

Pollyanna began to dance up and down lightly on her toes. "You didn't! You didn't say I *couldn't* do your hair, and that means that I may! Oh, I'm so glad!"

Pollyanna grabbed her aunt's hand and pulled her up the stairs. To her amazement, Aunt Polly soon found herself in the low chair before her dressing table, with her hair tumbling about her ears.

"Oh, my, what pretty hair you've got," exclaimed Pollyanna.

"Pollyanna! I'm sure I don't know why I'm letting you do this silly thing."

"I just love to do folks' hair," purred Pollyanna, working away. Pretty soon she said, "Now your hair is almost done, and I'm going to leave you for just a minute. And you must promise, promise, *promise* not to move till I come back!" And she ran from the room.

At that moment Miss Polly caught a glimpse of herself in the mirror. What she saw was a face glowing with excitement. Her cheeks were a pretty pink, her eyes sparkled, and her dark hair lay in loose waves about her forehead, with soft little curls here and there.

Before she could move, she felt something soft slipped over her shoulders. Pollyanna was draping about her aunt's shoulders a beautiful lace shawl she had found in the attic. Then she pulled her aunt toward the sunroom.

"Pollyanna, what are you doing? Where are you taking me to?"

"I'll have you ready now in no time," said Pollyanna, reaching for a red rose sitting in the vase and thrusting it into Miss Polly's soft hair. "There!" she cried. "Oh, Aunt Polly, now I reckon you'll be glad I dressed you up!"

Miss Polly looked at her reflection in the sunroom window. For the first time in years she liked what she saw. Then, all of a sudden, she gave a cry and fled to her room. Pollyanna turned and saw, through the window of the sunroom, Dr. Chilton's horse and carriage pulling into the driveway.

"Dr. Chilton, Dr. Chilton! Did you want to see me? I'm up here," Pollyanna called, throwing open the window to greet him.

"Yes," answered the doctor. "I've prescribed you for a patient, and he's sent me to get the prescription filled. Will you go?"

"I'd love to!" said Pollyanna. She went to say goodbye to Aunt Polly, but the door was closed and there was no answer when Pollyanna knocked.

So Pollyanna came down, and they started off. For some time Dr. Chilton said nothing. Then he asked, "Wasn't that your aunt I saw you with, in the window of the sunroom?"

Pollyanna sighed. "Yes. You see, I'd dressed her up in a perfectly lovely lace shawl, and I'd fixed her hair and put on a rose, and she looked so pretty. Did you see her? Didn't you think she looked just lovely?"

For a moment the doctor did not answer. "Yes, I thought she looked just lovely."

"Did you? I'm so glad! I'll tell her."

To her surprise the doctor suddenly cried, "Oh, no! Pollyanna, I'm afraid I shall have to ask you not to tell her that."

"Why, Dr. Chilton! I should think you'd be glad."

"But *she* might not be," cut in the doctor.

Pollyanna considered this for a moment. "That's so, maybe she wouldn't. It seemed that it was because she saw you that she ran."

"I thought as much," said the doctor, under his breath.

"Still, I don't see why, when she looked so pretty!"

The doctor said nothing, and he was quiet, indeed, all during Pollyanna's visit to Mr. Pendleton. On the return trip they stopped for a moment at Dr. Chilton's offices.

"I've never been to your home before!" said Pollyanna. "This is your home, isn't it?"

The doctor said, a little sadly, "Yes, but it's a pretty poor apology for a home, Pollyanna. They're just rooms, that's all, not a home."

Pollyanna nodded her head wisely. "I know. It takes a

woman's hand and heart, or a child's presence, to make a home," she said.

"Eh?" The doctor looked up at her.

"Why don't *you* get a woman's hand and heart, Dr. Chilton?"

There was a moment's silence. Then the doctor said, "They're not always to be had for the asking, little girl."

Pollyanna frowned. Then her eyes widened in surprise. "Why, Dr. Chilton, you don't mean that you *tried* to get somebody's hand and heart once, and couldn't, do you?"

The doctor got to his feet a little abruptly. "There, there, Pollyanna, never mind about that now. Let's get you back home."

But as they rode back, Pollyanna thought about Aunt Polly, and Dr. Chilton, and began to wonder.

[13]

An Accident

❖

IT WAS ON the last day of October that the accident occurred. Pollyanna, hurrying home from school, crossed the road at what looked like a safe distance in front of a motor car.

Just what happened, no one could tell afterward. Pollyanna, however, was carried unconscious into Miss Polly's house. There she was undressed and tenderly put to bed by her aunt and Nancy. They telephoned for Dr. Warren, who came as fast as he could.

There were no broken bones, but the doctor looked very grave, and he told Miss Polly that "time alone could tell."

It was not till the next morning that Pollyanna opened her eyes and realized where she was. "Why, Aunt Polly, what's happening? Is it daytime? Why am I in bed?" she cried. "Why, Aunt Polly, I can't get up!" she moaned, falling back on the pillow.

"No, dear, I wouldn't try just yet," soothed her aunt.

"But what is the matter? Why can't I get up?"

Aunt Polly cleared her throat and tried to explain. "You were hurt, dear, by the automobile yesterday. But never mind that now. Auntie wants you to rest and go to sleep again."

That day passed, and then another and another, with Pollyanna falling in and out of a feverish state. Finally, after a week, the fever broke for good, and she began to be more aware of her surroundings. She then had to be told all over again what had happened.

"So I'm hurt, and not sick," she sighed at last. "Well, I'm glad of that."

"Glad, Pollyanna?" asked her aunt, who was sitting by the bed.

"Yes. I'd so much rather have broken legs like Mr. Pendleton than be a lifelong invalid like Mrs. Snow, you know. Broken legs get well, and lifelong invalids don't."

Aunt Polly said nothing. She knew Pollyanna's legs were worse off than if they had been broken.

"I'm glad I don't have smallpox," Pollyanna continued. "That would be worse than freckles. And I'm glad it's not measles, because then you couldn't sit with me."

"You seem to be glad for a good many things, my dear," said Aunt Polly kindly.

"I am. I've been thinking of a good many of them. For example, since I've been hurt, you've called me 'dear' lots of times, and you didn't before. I love to be called 'dear.' Oh, Aunt Polly, I'm so glad you're here!"

Aunt Polly did not answer. Her eyes were too full of tears, so she went to sit alone for a moment in the parlor.

Dr. Warren had told Miss Polly that her niece's injury might be very serious. Pollyanna seemed to think that she just had a pair of broken legs, but if Dr. Warren were correct . . . but Miss Polly would not think about that.

Instead, she thought back to Pollyanna's arrival, and to her old ideas about duty. Miss Polly now realized that she no longer felt a sense of duty toward Pollyanna. What she felt was *love*.

14

Pollyanna's Diagnosis

❈

THE NEXT DAY Miss Polly had something to tell Pollyanna. "Dear," she began gently, "we have decided that we want another doctor besides Dr. Warren to see you. Another one might tell us something new to do, to help you get well faster."

A joyous light came to Pollyanna's face. "Oh, Aunt Polly, I'd so love to have Dr. Chilton! I've wanted him all the time, but I was afraid you didn't, on account of his seeing you in the sunroom that day. So I didn't like to say anything. But I'm so glad you do want him!"

Aunt Polly's face turned white, then red, then back to white again. "Oh, no, dear! It wasn't Dr. Chilton at all that I meant. It is a new doctor who knows a great deal about hurts like yours."

Pollyanna still looked unconvinced. "But, Aunt Polly, if you *loved* Dr. Chilton—"

"*What*, Pollyanna?" Miss Polly's face was beet-red now.

"I say, if you loved Dr. Chilton, and didn't love the other doctor, it seems to me that that might make a difference. And I love Dr. Chilton."

"I am very sorry, Pollyanna, but I'm afraid you'll have to let me be the judge this time. Besides, it's already arranged. Dr. Mead is coming tomorrow."

The next day Dr. Mead came. He was a tall, broad-shouldered man with kind gray eyes and a cheerful smile. Pollyanna liked him at once, and told him so.

"You look quite a lot like *my* doctor, you see," she said.

"*Your* doctor?" Dr. Mead looked over at Dr. Warren.

"Oh, *that* isn't my doctor," smiled Pollyanna. "Dr. Warren is Aunt Polly's doctor. My doctor is Dr. Chilton. But Aunt Polly said you knew more than Dr. Chilton about broken legs like mine. And of course, if you do, I can be glad for that. Do you?"

"Only time can tell that, little girl," he said gently, and began to examine her.

When he was through, Dr. Mead went into the hall to speak privately with Dr. Warren and Aunt Polly.

Everyone said that what happened next was the cat's fault. If Fluffy had not pressed her nose against Pollyanna's closed door, it would not have swung noiselessly open on its hinges. And if the door had not been open, Pollyanna would not have heard her aunt's words.

"Not that! Doctor, not that! You don't mean—the child will *never* walk again!"

It was all confusion then. First, from the bedroom came Pollyanna's terrified "Aunt Polly, Aunt Polly!" Then Aunt Polly, seeing the open door and realizing that her words had been heard, gave a low moan and fainted dead away.

Dr. Mead caught Aunt Polly as she fell, while Dr. Warren went into Pollyanna's room.

"Dr. Warren, please, I want Aunt Polly. I want her right away, quick, please!"

"She can't come just this minute, dear. She will, a little later. What is it? Can't I get it?"

"I want to know what she said just now. Did you hear her? I want Aunt Polly. I want her to tell me it isn't true!"

Dr. Warren, against his better judgment, found himself saying, "Perhaps Dr. Mead was mistaken, dear. There are a lot of things that can happen, you know."

"But Aunt Polly said he *did* know! She said he knew more than anybody else about broken legs like mine!"

"Yes, I know, dear. But we doctors make mistakes sometimes. Just don't think anymore about it now."

Pollyanna flung out her arms wildly. "But I can't help thinking about it. It's all there is now to think about. Why, if I can't walk, how am I ever going to be glad for *anything*?"

Dr. Warren did not know the game. But he did know that his patient must be quieted, and at once. So he prepared a sleeping powder for the girl.

"There, there, dear, just take this," he soothed. "And by and by you'll be more rested, and we'll see what can be done then. Things aren't half as bad as they seem, dear, lots of times."

Obediently Pollyanna took the medicine.

"I know. That sounds like things Father used to say," said Pollyanna, blinking away her tears. "He said there was always something about everything that might be worse. But he'd never heard that he couldn't ever walk again. I don't see how there can be anything worse than that, do you?"

Dr. Warren could not reply. He just watched Pollyanna drift off into sleep.

15

Messages

❦

IT WAS NANCY who went to tell Mr. John Pendleton the news. When he came to the door, she said, "Miss Polly sent me to tell you about Miss Pollyanna."

"Well?" said Mr. Pendleton, with a worried look.

"It's not good," she choked.

"You don't mean—" He paused, and she bowed her head.

"Yes, sir. Dr. Mead says she can't walk again, ever."

"Poor little girl! Poor little girl!" he cried. "It seems so cruel that she'll never dance in the sunshine again!" There was a silence, and then he asked, "She doesn't know yet, does she?"

"But she does, sir," sobbed Nancy. "And that's what makes it all the harder. She overheard Miss Polly talking with the doctor."

"Poor little girl!" sighed Mr. Pendleton again.

"It worries her, too, that she can't be glad. But maybe you don't know about her game."

"The Glad Game?" he asked. "Oh, yes. She's told me of that."

"Oh, she did! Well, I guess she has told it to almost everybody in town. But you see, now she can't play it herself, and it worries her. She says she can't think of a thing to be glad about."

"Well, why should she?" asked Mr. Pendleton.

"That's the way I felt, too, till I happened to think. It *would* be easier if she could find something to be glad about, you know. So I tried to remind her."

"To remind her! Of what?"

"Of how she told others to play it. But she says it's easier to *tell* lifelong invalids how to be glad than it is to actually *be* glad."

Nancy paused, but the man could not speak.

"Then I tried to remind her how she used to say the game was nicer to play when it was hard. But she says it's different when it's *too* hard. Well, I must be going now, sir," she said, leaving Mr. Pendleton teary-eyed.

It did not take long for the entire town to learn that the doctor had said Pollyanna would never walk again. In kitchens and in sitting rooms and over backyard fences, men and women wept openly. And it became even worse when they learned that poor Pollyanna could not play her game, and that she could not now be glad over anything.

It was then that Miss Polly began to receive calls from what seemed like the entire town. And the odd thing was, so many of the messages left for Pollyanna sounded very much the same.

"Please tell Miss Pollyanna that I'm so *glad* that I've started to knit again," was the message that Mrs. Snow sent.

"Do let the little girl know how *glad* I am that the sun has been shining all week," was in a note from Mr. Pendleton.

"Tell her we're so *glad* that Mother will be visiting next week," came from a woman whom Miss Polly had never even met.

These messages seemed to raise Pollyanna's spirits mightily, but Miss Polly was mystified. "Pollyanna, what is the meaning of all these messages? Why does everyone insist that they are so glad about everything?"

"Oh, isn't it lovely, Aunt Polly?" cried Pollyanna quickly. "They're all playing the Glad Game! Father would be so happy! He'd—" But Pollyanna stopped abruptly, remembering that she wasn't to speak about her father to Aunt Polly. So she tried to change the subject.

"I'm a little concerned about Dr. Chilton, Aunt Polly. I don't think he's at all happy. He needs a woman's hand and heart, I believe."

Miss Polly's face flushed. "Dr. Chilton! How do you know *that*?"

"He told me so—that is, before the accident. So I asked him why he didn't get them—a woman's hand and heart—and have a home."

"What did he say?" Miss Polly asked breathlessly.

"He didn't say anything for a minute. Then he said that you couldn't always get them for the asking. Why, Aunt Polly, what's wrong?" Aunt Polly had hurried to the window.

"Nothing, dear," she said, but she would not turn around.

The next day Miss Polly went to see Nancy in the kitchen. "Nancy, will you tell me what this absurd game is that the whole town seems to be babbling about? And what, please, has my niece to do with it? Why does everybody send word to her that they're glad? I tried to ask the child herself about it, but I can't seem to make much headway."

"It means that ever since June that child has been making the whole town glad, and now they're trying to make her a little glad, too."

"Glad of what?"

"Just glad! That's the game."

Miss Polly actually stamped her foot. "There you go like all the rest, Nancy. *What* game?"

So Nancy described the care package, and the crutches, and the game that Pollyanna and her father played.

"Well, I know somebody else who'll play it now," said Miss Polly as she turned and went to Pollyanna's room.

"Pollyanna, I wanted to tell you how glad I am to be able to spend so much time with you lately. I wish you weren't hurt, of course, but I'm still so *glad* that we can chat with each other."

Pollyanna looked up quickly. "Why, Aunt Polly, you spoke just as if you knew about the game. *Do* you know about the game, Aunt Polly?"

"Yes, dear," Miss Polly said. "Nancy told me. I think it's a beautiful game, and after you've told me all about how your father taught it to you, I'm going to play it with you."

"Oh, Aunt Polly, *you*? I'm so glad! I've really wanted you most of anybody, all the time. And I'm so glad I can talk about my father to you, too!"

16

Dr. Chilton's Dilemma

❖

THE WINTER PASSED, and spring came. There was little change in Pollyanna's condition. There seemed every reason to believe that the girl would never walk again.

In the town one man in particular fretted and fumed over Pollyanna's condition. As the days passed and the news grew no better, he decided he *had* to do something. That's why, one Saturday morning, Mr. Pendleton received a visit from Dr. Chilton.

"Mr. Pendleton," began the doctor. "I've come to ask a favor of you. I want to see that child, and I want to make an examination. I *must* make an examination."

"Well, why can't you?" asked Mr. Pendleton.

"Why can't I? Well, because many years ago—fifteen, in fact—Miss Polly Harrington forbade me to enter her house."

"But why?"

"We . . . We. . . ." the doctor faltered. "We were engaged to be married! But we had a spat. Miss Polly told me that the *next* time she *asked* me to enter her house, it would mean she was begging my pardon, and that she would consent to marry me. So you see, she won't call for me now!"

"Chilton, what *was* the quarrel about?" asked Mr. Pendleton.

"Nothing of any importance. So far as I am concerned, I am willing to say there was no quarrel. But I must see that child. I honestly believe that if I see her, then chances are Pollyanna will walk again!"

"Walk! What do you mean?"

"I mean that from what I hear, her case is very much like one that a college friend of mine has just helped. I must see the girl!"

"Then *I* shall convince Miss Polly, Chilton!"

Mr. Pendleton left immediately to see Miss Polly. She had no sooner understood what he was saying than she begged for Dr. Chilton to come at once.

"You are inviting him to your home then?" asked Mr. Pendleton.

"Yes, indeed I am," answered Miss Polly.

"But your pledge to him?"

Miss Polly just blushed and looked out the window to await the arrival of Dr. Chilton.

66

17

And What Came Next

❖

THE VERY NEXT day a broad-shouldered man came into Pollyanna's room.

"Dr. Chilton! Oh, Dr. Chilton, how glad I am to see you!" cried Pollyanna. "But, of course, if Aunt Polly doesn't want——"

"It is all right, my dear. Don't worry," soothed Aunt Polly, hurrying forward. "I have told Dr. Chilton that I want him to look you over this morning."

"Oh, then you *asked* him to come," murmured Pollyanna.

"Yes, dear, I asked him. That is——" But it was too late. The question that had leaped to Dr. Chilton's eyes was unmistakable, and Miss Polly had seen it. And her own eyes answered his—yes.

Dr. Chilton held out both his hands to Pollyanna. "Little girl, I think you've done one of your very gladdest jobs today, though you didn't know it." Then he examined the girl thoroughly.

At twilight a wonderfully different Aunt Polly crept to Pollyanna's bedside. "Pollyanna, dear, I'm going to tell you some special news. Someday soon Dr. Chilton is going to be your uncle. And it's you who have done it all. Oh, Pollyanna, I'm so happy! And I'm so glad, darling!"

Pollyanna began to clap her hands. "Aunt Polly, were *you* the woman's hand and heart he wanted so long ago? You *were*, I know you were! And that's what he meant by saying I'd done the gladdest job of all today. I'm so glad! Why, I'm so glad that I don't even mind my legs now!"

Aunt Polly did not yet want to tell Pollyanna the great hope that Dr. Chilton had given her. But she did say this: "Pollyanna, next week you're going to take a journey, to a great doctor, who has a big house made on purpose for people who've had accidents like yours. He's a dear friend of Dr. Chilton's, and we're going to see what he can do for you!"

18

Pollyanna's Letter

❖

Dear Aunt Polly and Uncle Tom,

Oh, I can *walk*! I did today all the way from my bed to the window! It was six steps. My, how good it was to be on legs again!

All the doctors stood around and smiled, and all the nurses stood beside them and cried. I don't see why they cried. I wanted to sing and shout and yell! Oh! Just think, I can walk, *walk*, WALK! Now I don't mind having been here almost ten months, and I'm so glad I didn't miss the wedding. Wasn't that just like you, Aunt Polly, to come *here* and get married right beside my bed, so I could see you.

Pretty soon, they say, I shall go home. I wish I could walk all the way there! Oh, I'm so glad! I'm glad for everything. Why, I'm glad now I lost my legs for a while, for you never know how perfectly lovely legs are till you haven't got them. I'm going to walk at *least* eight steps tomorrow.

With heaps of love to everybody,
Pollyanna